TWEED SERIES

CHOOSE YOUR OWN ADVENTURE®
titles in Large-Print Editions:

All-Time Best-Sellers!

CHOOSE YOUR OWN ADVENTURE® • 88

MASTER OF KUNG FU

BY RICHARD BRIGHTFIELD

ILLUSTRATED BY FRANK BOLLE

An Edward Packard Book

Gareth Stevens Publishing
MILWAUKEE

For a free color catalog describing Gareth Stevens' list of high-quality books, call 1-800-542-2595 (USA) or 1-800-461-9120 (Canada). Gareth Stevens' Fax: (414) 225-0377.

Library of Congress Cataloging-in-Publication Data available upon request from publisher.
Fax: (414) 225-0377 for the attention of the Publishing Records Department.

ISBN 0-8368-1309-X

This edition first published in 1995 by
Gareth Stevens Publishing
1555 North RiverCenter Drive, Suite 201
Milwaukee, Wisconsin 53212 USA

CHOOSE YOUR OWN ADVENTURE® is a trademark of Bantam Doubleday Dell Books for Young Readers, a division of Bantam Doubleday Dell Publishing Group, Inc.

Original conception of Edward Packard.
Interior illustrations by Frank Bolle. Cover art by David Mattingly.

1 2 3 4 5 6 7 8 9 99 98 97 96 95

Printed in the United States of America

For Charles Kochman

WARNING!!!

Do not read this book straight through from beginning to end. These pages contain many different adventures that you may have when you travel to China for a kung fu tour with your best friend. From time to time as you read along, you will be asked to make a choice. Your choice may lead to success or disaster!

Each adventure you take is the result of your choice. You are responsible because you choose! After you make a choice, follow the instructions to see what happens to you next.

Think carefully before you make a decision. Young tourists visiting China have been vanishing mysteriously. If you don't find your best friend soon, you may spend your entire vacation fighting against Ninja—alone!

Good luck!

You can hardly believe it. It's the first time you've ever flown, and here you are on a jumbo jet thousands of feet above the Pacific Ocean—on your way to China!

Your best friend, Billy, is seated next to you. Thanks to him, you'll be spending this month of your summer vacation in China.

Billy's a martial arts nut. His kung fu school arranged a tour of China for his martial arts class, and you managed to talk your parents into letting you come, too, even though you haven't been studying kung fu.

Billy spends most of the flight telling you about China and kung fu. "The Shao-lin Temple in central China is where kung fu all got started," Billy says excitedly, filling the air with kung fu and karate chops.

Turn to page 11.

2

You supervise the reinforcement of the walls that protect the city.

Unfortunately you've underestimated the enemy's strength. They attack and capture one wall after another. Finally they enter the palace itself, and you are forced to flee. The emperor is captured, but Lin Fu escapes with you to the south.

When it is certain that the empire is lost, Lin Fu goes into hiding with you at the Shao-lin Temple. There you live out the rest of your life in its peaceful gardens.

The End

The cab inches along through the crowd, behind a rumbling trolley car.

"Is it always like this?" you ask the cabdriver.

"Nanjing Road all the time very busy," the driver shouts over the din. "Many miles long, many shops."

Finally you reach the Peace Hotel. You pay the cab driver with your Chinese yuan and hope he gives you the right change.

The tour doesn't begin till tomorrow morning, so after you check into the hotel and drop off your bags, you rush back outside, anxious to explore Shanghai.

Billy, his camera slung over his shoulder, studies a street map. "There should be a photo shop around here somewhere," he says. "I want to find out how long it takes to get film developed."

"Let's go," you say enthusiastically, fascinated by the hustle and bustle of Shanghai.

Turn to page 4.

4

Nanjing Road is still teeming with bicycle riders and people. You are trying to cross the road when Billy is almost run down by a bicycle. As he jumps back, you see someone in the crowd snatch the camera off his shoulder.

"Hey! Stop!" Billy shouts, and plunges into the crowd after the thief, who is now running down a side street.

"Wait for me," you yell. But Billy is already out of sight. You push through the crowd, but you've lost him.

You run in the direction that Billy and the thief went. You see Billy at the end of the block, across the street, standing in the doorway of a shop.

"Billy! Wait!" You shout and wave your hands.

Billy stops and turns in your direction at the same time as a trolley car passes in front of you.

The trolley passes and—he's gone!

Turn to page 12.

6

Ling and the captain go forward. Chun Li shouts orders to a group of sailors. They pull up the gangplank, and you feel the ship moving, its engines throbbing beneath you.

The ship steams up the muddy river and out of Shanghai. It enters a wider and a muddier river, the Yangtze. As the sun rises, everything is enveloped in a yellow fog.

A few hours later, the air clears. Now you have left the river and are well out to sea.

You are resting near the bow when you hear shouts from the stern of the ship. You go to the stern and see pairs of kung fu fighters dressed in loose-fitting costumes with black sashes at the waist. The fighters are engaged in mock combat, some with bare hands and others with swords or knives.

Turn to page 15.

Suddenly a shout goes up from several of the Ninja as they point to the shore. Kung fu fighters are on the beach and charging toward you. You see Ling and the man who rescued you in the Shanghai courtyard a few days before.

The Ninja take fighting stances, and seconds later the Ninja and the kung fu fighters connect in a wild melee of flashing hands and feet. The Ninja fight desperately, but they are no match for the kung fu fighters.

You see the Ninja leader retreating toward the barracks. Springing into action, you bring him down from behind with a flying snap kick that you learned from Ling.

After all the Ninja are subdued and sitting on the ground in a circle, Ling approaches you. "We follow you here. You bait," she says sheepishly. "We put electronic bug in shoe when you sleep at night in Shanghai."

Turn to page 41.

You and Billy leave the plane and enter a modern airport terminal. Officials check your passports as you move through customs. Then you exchange your American money for some strange-looking Chinese money called *yuan.*

Outside the terminal, you hail a "Red Flag" taxi. It looks like a large 1950s Buick, but it's actually made in China.

"You Americans?" the driver, who is wearing a NY Yankees baseball cap, asks you. "I speak very good English. Where to, boss?"

Billy looks at the piece of paper the travel agent gave him back home. "The Peace Hotel on Nanjing Road," he says.

"Hun hao," says the driver. "Peace Hotel— very good."

You grip the edge of your seat as the cab speeds away from the airport and toward the hub of the city, about fifteen miles away.

You arrive at a vast checkerboard of low, white-washed houses and boxy apartment buildings. The taxi barrels around a corner into a honey-comb of narrow streets and screeches to a stop.

You stare in amazement at the chaos in the street, thick with bicycles. The riders are all jingling their bicycle bells, and radio loudspeakers blasting from all directions add to the terrific din.

Turn to page 3.

10

"I'd like to go to Hong Kong," you say.

"Good," says Chang Li, slapping you on the shoulder. "We have many friends who will help you. In fact, there is a freighter leaving in the morning that can take you. My granddaughter, Ling, is also going.

Chang Li leads you to a small, clean room with a single bed. "You can sleep here," he says, and quietly closes the door behind you.

You take your shoes off and crawl into bed. You don't realize how tired you are until you lie down. You fall asleep immediately.

In the morning, you wake to a gentle knock at the door. You open the door and Ling enters. "Eat now. We go soon," she says, placing a tray with small cakes and a cup of hot tea on a small table near your bed.

You eat hungrily, relieved to see that they don't eat insects for breakfast. You are just tying your shoes when Ling knocks again to tell you it's time to go.

The two of you set off for the freighter in the faint gray light of the early dawn. Soon you arrive at a dock.

You and Ling walk up the gangplank onto an old rusty freighter. A short, stocky man meets you on the deck. He greets Ling enthusiastically in Chinese.

"This Chun Li, captain of ship," Ling tells you. "I explain him everything."

Turn to page 6.

"Another really interesting thing about China, Japan, and the Orient is the Ninja," Billy tells you as he pulls out a book and points to a picture. "The Ninja spent years training to become assassins. They were masters of kung fu and all the other martial arts, too. They also knew how to use a lot of different weapons, poison, trickery, disguise, hypnotism, and even magic."

"Are we going to meet Ninja on the tour?" you ask.

"Of course not," says Billy, playfully punching your arm. "That's all ancient history. There aren't any Ninja anymore."

Finally, exhausted from talking, you lie back in your seat and daydream about the Great Wall of China, the Forbidden City, the Imperial Palace, even panda bears.

"Please fasten your seat belts," says the flight attendant, gently shaking your arm. "We're about to land."

You lean toward the window to look for Shanghai airport and see the city below you. A river lined with large buildings snakes through the center of it.

You brace yourself and cross your fingers as the plane touches down. With a squeal of the brakes, it comes to a stop.

Turn to page 9.

12

You run to the doorway where Billy was standing. It's the entrance to a photo store.

You walk in and look around. It takes a moment for your eyes to adjust to the dim light. You see a wooden shelf lined with cameras—one of them looks like Billy's!

You are startled when a small Chinese woman suddenly appears out of the shadows. She is dressed in a blue silk dress with a high collar. "You want to buy camera?" she asks.

"No," you answer. "I'm looking for my friend. I think he just came in here."

"No see anyone. Here all time," she says.

Disappointed and confused, you return to the hotel.

There's no sign of Billy at the hotel, and he doesn't return that night.

In the morning, you pack your bag and go to the tour office, hoping that Billy will meet you there. In the office you see a muscular, middle-aged man looking at a clipboard. You introduce yourself.

He shakes your hand vigorously. "Hi, I'm Robert Cole. I'm your tour guide. You can call me Bob."

Go on to the next page.

"Glad to meet you, Bob," you say. "Can you tell me if Billy Richards has shown up yet?"

Bob checks his clipboard and shakes his head. "Nope, haven't seen him." Bob glances quickly at his watch. "All aboard!" he yells.

You watch in dismay as everyone boards the bus.

"Can't you wait for him?" you ask in desperation.

"Sorry. Can't do that." Bob shrugs apologetically. "If we don't leave right now, we may miss our connection. Are you coming?"

*If you stay in Shanghai to look for Billy,
turn to page 24.*

*If you board the bus and hope Billy will catch
up with the tour, turn to page 34.*

You watch as Ling flies through the air and does a double somersault to escape the blow of her opponent. Ling sees you and beckons you to join them.

"You wish to know kung fu?" she asks.

"Sure," you say, eager to learn.

Ling teaches you the basics of kung fu: how to stand, kicking techniques, fist blows and fan blocks. At the end of the session you are getting the hang of it and really enjoying yourself. No wonder Billy is so into kung fu, you think.

Turn to page 20.

16

"Thank you very much for helping me, but I think I'll go back to the hotel," you tell the man.

"Must leave quickly, then. Men return with others. Maybe we meet again," he says, and bows. He disappears into the night.

You hear a door creak open on the opposite side of the court. Without waiting to see who it is, you run out of the courtyard and keep running until your lungs feel as if they're about to burst. Finally you stop to catch your breath. You walk down another side street that leads you back to Jiangsu Road.

Turn to page 27.

You follow the man as he hurries outside. He opens the back door of a Red Flag taxi for you, and you jump in. He slams the door shut and gets in the driver's seat. There is a heavy glass partition between the two of you.

The taxi speeds away from the hotel. You smell something funny.

There's gas hissing into the backseat!

You try to jump out of the cab, but the back doors are locked, and there are no handles on the inside.

You are beginning to feel dizzy, and you can't breathe.

The last thing you see is the man in the front seat leering at you through the glass partition.

The End

18

You follow Chang Li and Ling inside and down a long hallway paneled in dark, elaborately carved wood. Chang Li opens a wide door and leads you into a large room with red and green walls. In the center of the room is a circular dining table with large steaming bowls of food. More than a dozen people—men, women, and children—are seated around it. Chang Li points to some empty seats at the end. You, Chang Li, and Ling sit down at the table.

"Very good food," he says. "We have steamed boa constrictor, fried ants, live baby eels, noodles, and for dessert, chilled monkey brains. Delicious!" He sits at the table and hungrily picks up a pair of chopsticks.

You stare at the pot of squirming eels. "Ah, Mr. Li, perhaps I could have a peanut butter sandwich instead?" you ask, hoping you aren't being rude to your host, who is already wolfing down his food.

"Sorry, no peanut butter," Chang Li says, happily munching his fried ants.

He notices that you are not eating. "What's the matter, you not hungry? Food not good enough for you?" he asks, putting down his chopsticks and wiping a noodle off his chin.

The rest of the people at the table stop eating. They all look at you.

Turn to page 28.

20

That night you sleep peacefully on the deck of the freighter. In the morning the freighter passes through the narrows into Hong Kong harbor.

Ling hands you a slip of paper with an address on it. "You go," she says. "Wait till we call."

You take a taxi to a small hotel. You pick up your key at the small front desk and find your way to your room.

Just as you lie down on your bed to wait for Ling's call, the phone rings.

That was quick, you think to yourself as you pick up the phone, expecting to hear Ling's melodic voice.

"Hello. Is that you?" a voice asks. Your heart skips a beat. It's Billy!

"Billy! Where are you?" you ask frantically.

"It's a long story," he says. "I can't talk now. Just meet me at Ocean Park—by the sharks. Tonight!" Billy hangs up before you have the chance to say anything.

If you go to meet Billy, turn to page 30.

If you wait for Ling to call, turn to page 106.

"Excuse me, Mr. Li," you say. "I don't mean any disrespect, but—could I cut the grass later? I just want to find my friend!" You struggle to control your frustration. "Do you know where Billy is or not?"

"Friend in Hong Kong," Chang Li says abruptly.

"Hong Kong!" You stop walking in the garden, bewildered. "What . . . how did he get there? Who took . . . ?"

"Ninja!" The word bursts from Chang Li's mouth, as if he were spitting out a piece of rice stuck between his teeth.

You stare, speechless, at Chang Li. "What should I do now, Mr. Li?"

"Go to Hong Kong. Find friend," he says simply.

If you decide to go to Hong Kong, turn to page 10.

If you decide to go back to the hotel, turn to page 104.

The next few weeks are a blur. The only thing you clearly understand is that you're being trained to be a Ninja assassin!

At the end of your training, you are lined up for instructions by the Ninja leader.

"All of you are now ready for missions in your own countries. When the time is right, I will instruct you to assassinate the leaders of your countries.

"Then I will be Master of the World!"

Even though you despise what you're being trained to do, you are powerless to resist.

The End

24

You watch as the tour bus vanishes into the traffic down the block. You wait at the tour office, hoping that Billy will show up eventually. But after a few hours, you decide to go back to the hotel to check if Billy has left a message for you there.

You walk back to the hotel and go to the front desk.

"Did my friend Billy leave a message for me while I was out?" you ask politely.

The clerk checks the boxes behind him, but there's nothing there for you.

"Oh, well." You sigh. You'd better hang around in case Billy comes back, you decide. "I think I'll stay here for a few more days and join my tour later," you tell the clerk at the front desk.

"So sorry, hotel booked up. Find you room another place," he says, picking up the phone and making a few phone calls.

He writes on a slip of paper: Flowery Hotel, Jiangsu Road.

You pick up your bag from your room and ask the clerk to keep Billy's suitcase here at the hotel for now. Then you take a cab to the Flowery Hotel.

An elderly woman grabs your sleeve as you walk through the doorway. "You must be young man Mr. Wu said was coming," the woman says.

Turn to page 58.

You pretend to eat, smiling at some of the people sitting near you. No one speaks as they shovel the food into their mouths, barely chewing before they swallow. You notice that the others are beginning to get glassy eyed. The food must be drugged!

"Everyone up!" a Ninja orders after the food is gone. The prisoners snap out of their lethargy and jump to their feet. You do the same.

"Follow me!" he orders. Everyone follows in a single file out of the barracks onto a drill field.

Turn to page 37.

It's dark when you get back to the hotel. You go up to your room, lock your door, and throw yourself down on your mattress. Just as you are wondering where to look for Billy next, you hear three sharp raps on your door. You cautiously walk to the door and open it a crack.

A small Chinese girl with long black pigtails, dressed in faded blue jeans and a pink silk mandarin jacket, is standing there.

She bows. "Please come with me," she says.

Puzzled, you wonder where she came from. China sure is a land full of mystery, you think. You hope this isn't a trick, because you need all the help you can get. You decide to go with the girl.

Turn to page 35.

28

"It looks great," you say, trying to pick up a piece of boa constrictor with your chopsticks. "It's just that—uh—I'm really worried because my friend has disappeared."

"Eat now, talk later," Chang Li says, happily returning to his meal.

You watch, horrified, as Chang Li sucks the insides out of a roasted beetle. He licks his lips and uses his sleeve to wipe a beetle leg off his chin. Your stomach is turning, but you manage to swallow two pieces of boa constrictor and five fried ants.

After the others finish eating, you walk with Chang Li into a lotus blossom garden.

Chang Li says, "Your life is like a blade of grass, pushing its way through the ground. The beginning will be met with much difficulty. Your life is now just beginning. You must grow and not lose hope. Then you will achieve your goal, just as the grass reaches for the sun."

Turn to page 21.

Surprised, you slip back through the trapdoor, hanging by your fingers, half in and half out. The figure leans toward you. Behind you are several others.

They are dressed in white kung fu tunics with black sashes around their waist.

One of them reaches down and pulls you up into the room.

"Glad to find you," he says. "We worry about foreign guest."

They throw down a rope for Billy and pull him out.

When you and Billy are safe, the kung fu leader introduces himself and explains, "You the victim of Ninja plot. Ninja kidnapping young kung fu fighters. Then they hypnotize fighters and train to be assassins."

"Assassins!" you and Billy cry in alarm.

"That was a close one," says Billy.

"Next vacation," you say to Billy, "let's just go canoeing!"

The End

30

Billy could be in trouble and need your help, you think, rushing from your room and out of the hotel. After a few tries, you find a traffic cop who speaks English. He gives you directions to Ocean Park.

When you get there, you buy a ticket and quickly find the shark house. You walk inside looking around for Billy. It's dark inside the building, but there is a luminous glass wall stretching from one side of the house to the other. Several huge sharks circle lazily in the translucent water.

Then you see Billy.

"Billy!" you shout. You run to your friend and grab him, excited and relieved that you have found him at last.

His face is oddly expressionless.

Suddenly two figures burst out of the darkness. One of them grabs your neck and presses down hard. You start to scream in pain as you feel your body collapse to the ground.

Turn to page 38.

32

Early the next morning, you start on horseback toward the capital of the empire. After two days of riding across the flat wide plains of central China, you come to the "water country" with its many streams, lakes, and rivers.

You leave your horse with a farmer, and a fisherman ferries you across the wide river.

As the sun sets, you reach the high, massive wall that surrounds the capital. You approach a gate, but it's locked. The gate guard explains that the only way into the city after sunset is by the "night basket." For a small fee, you can be hauled by a rope more than fifty feet straight up to the top of the wall.

You wonder if you should wait till morning when you could slip inside with a crowd of people. After all, you'll be a sitting duck in that basket if your enemies spot you. On the other hand, it's a moonless night, and there's no one else around.

If you use the night basket, turn to page 43.

If you decide to wait until morning, turn to page 105.

You accept the post as commander in chief of the emperor's forces. A war council is called with twenty of the top generals and the emperor presiding. Lin Fu is also there.

One of the generals comes forward. "Your Highness," he says, bowing low to the emperor, "we are experimenting with a new secret weapon. We call it the 'fire-spitting lance.' It's a long bamboo tube; one end is filled with exploding powder and sealed. When the powder is ignited, it shoots metal pellets out the other end. We have already made many of these. With their use, we can defeat our enemies.

"Bah," says another of the generals. "We do not have sufficient troops to fight their horsemen with or without this "fire lance." The enemy can shoot their arrows accurately at full gallop. We must strengthen our defenses inside the palace walls before it is too late!"

The emperor turns to you. "You must decide which is the better plan," he says.

If you decide on an immediate attack,
turn to page 113.

If you decide on strengthening the defenses,
turn to page 2.

You wait until the last possible second but then get on the bus. You look out the window, hoping you'll see Billy running down the street.

The bus winds its way through the streets of Shanghai. Twenty minutes later, it stops in front of a massive stone building.

"Everyone out for the train," Bob shouts. He jumps off first and leads the tour group through the crowded station and onto the train.

Fifteen minutes later, a whistle screeches. The train, pulled by an old-fashioned chugging steam engine, moves out of the station.

The train stops often, and you buy donuts, tea, and slices of watermelon from the local people who are selling food from small carts on the railroad platform.

Finally Bob comes through your train car and announces that the group is getting off at the next stop.

The train is met by a rickety old bus, and the group climbs aboard. The bus bounces down a dirt road, then up into the foothills of a mountain range. After several hours, it stops in front of an elegant one-story gatehouse. Its curving tiled roof is topped by a row of gilded ornaments.

"This is the entrance to the Shao-lin Temple," Bob says. The tour group bows respectfully.

Turn to page 63.

You follow the girl down the stairs and out to the street. Now it's really dark. A few shops are dimly lit. Street lamps create widely spaced pools of light—about one to a block. The streets are still crowded, though not as much as during the day.

The girl moves quickly, looking back every once in a while to make sure you're still behind her. You come to a river and cross a high, arching bridge that leads you into an even darker part of the city.

You're beginning to wonder if going with the girl was a good idea after all. She could be leading you right into an ambush. You shudder at the thought and are about to run back into the main part of the city when the girl leads you into a small courtyard, illuminated by a single small lantern.

A door opens on the ground floor of one of the buildings and throws a shaft of light across the courtyard. An ancient-looking Chinese gentleman with a long thin gray beard stands silhouetted in the doorway.

"Ah, welcome to House of Yi Lung Tong, home and training ground for secret freedom fighters, enemies of Ninja. I am your humble servant, Chang Li." He bows. "And this is my grand-daughter, Ling." Ling also bows. You bow back, awkwardly.

Turn to page 18.

You are surrounded by black-suited Ninja. You glance at the Ninja who is guarding you. It's Billy! You want to ask him what's going on, but you're afraid the other Ninja might realize you're not really drugged after all.

The Ninja leader faces you and the other captives. "You have all been chosen for your potential ability in the martial arts and for your country of origin," he says. "You will be trained to be Ninja assassins. Then you will be hypnotized and forget you were ever here and what you have learned—until I decide the time is right! Then you will receive a code word that will activate your mission—to assassinate the leaders of your countries. This will enable me to seize world power!"

Turn to page 7.

When you wake up, your vision is blurred. You see a face looking down at you. It looks exactly like the picture Billy showed you on the plane. It's a Ninja!

The Ninja herds you and several other captives into a barracks building. You notice that the captives are of many different nationalities. Everyone sits around a long square table. In front of you are plates of food.

"Everyone eat!" orders the Ninja.

You're ravenous, and the food looks good.

Then you remember Billy's blank expression when you saw him back at the Shark House. Maybe the food is poisoned!

If you eat the food, turn to page 92.

If you only pretend to eat, turn to page 25.

Before you can react to the man with the knife, a piercing cry comes from above as a figure hurls down from one of the balconies. A foot flashes past you, knocking the knife out of the attacker's hand. He snarls like a wounded tiger, turns toward your rescuer, and crouches in a fighting stance.

Another lightning kick catches your attacker in the head. He tumbles into a backward somersault, coming up again in a fighting crouch.

There is a blur of action as your rescuer spins in the air, and several men fall to the ground, caught by blows that were too fast for you to see.

But there are so many against *one!* A man rushes him with a short spear, but you manage to tackle the spear carrier, and the weapon goes flying into the foot of another man who is about to deliver a kick to the head of your protecter. Then your friend gets off a series of fast blows, knocking out several men at once.

The attackers seem to have had enough, and they all disappear back through the doors.

"Do you speak English?" you ask the stranger, after he's caught his breath.

"Little English; not very good," he answers.

"How did you get here?" you ask him.

"Follow same man as you," he says.

"Why did they attack me?" you ask.

"They think you me?" he says. "Must leave quickly. Follow me, I take you to safe place."

If you follow him, turn to page 61.

If you decide to return to the hotel, turn to page 16.

40

"Is this some kind of joke?" you ask the monks. But they don't seem to hear your question.

"Are you all right?" asks one of the monks.

"I think so," you reply.

"You fall and hit head, but all right now," the monk says. "The master is waiting for you in the great hall. Good luck. We hope you graduate to the highest order of the Shao-lin Temple."

Confused and groggy, you walk to the great hall.

Inside the hall is a vast, high-ceilinged room. The floor is a wide expanse of dark polished wood. You file in with other young monks and sit cross-legged in front of the Grand Master.

Seated on a raised platform, the master leads everyone in a period of silent meditation.

Am I dreaming, or have I somehow gone back into the past? you wonder as you meditate.

The master rings a hand-held bell and calls your name. Confused, you stand up and go forward, bowing respectfully to the master.

It's bizarre, but your body seems to have a mind of its own. You unwrap your orange robe. Underneath you are wearing a white kung fu tunic. Several of the other monks do the same. They surround you and take fighting stances.

Then they attack you!

Turn to page 44.

You're happy to be rescued but still worried about Billy. "That one's not a real Ninja," you say, pointing to Billy, tied up with the rest of the Ninja. "He's my friend that was kidnapped a few days ago—"

"We know," she interrupts. "No worry, he be all right. He just drugged. Soon drug wear off."

Ling walks over to Billy, unties him, and helps him to his feet. She shakes him gently.

Billy mumbles something about getting a new camera and the kung fu tour.

"What friend needs," Ling says, "is good rest."

And that's what you both take—when you get home.

The End

You flip the guard a small coin and climb into the rickety basket. It's just large enough to hold you. You nervously yank the rope attached to it—the signal to be pulled up.

The guard pulls on a rope, and you begin to rise *very* slowly. The basket stops several times, dangling you precariously in the night air.

Have you been spotted by spies?

Turn to page 54.

44

You fend off the monks with lightninglike thrusts, fist strikes, elbow strikes, and kicks that come to you naturally, as if you had practiced them every day for years.

You counter all five opponents' blows effortlessly—and then aggressively attack your opponents.

Suddenly the Grand Master rings the bell. The monks return to their places. The Grand Master presents you with a bronze scepter. You are now a master of kung fu!

"Time to leave temple," the Grand Master says to you. "You must choose one of two vital missions. The first is to go to the court of the emperor and prevent his assassination! The second is to go to the western provinces and protect the foreigners there. China must be made safe for trade, or China always live in past."

It's hard for you to decide. Either choice is full of danger.

On the other hand—you're now a master of kung fu!

If you go to the court of the emperor,
turn to page 32.

If you go to the western provinces,
turn to page 70.

You follow the man. He walks briskly down the street, gliding through the crowd. You have a hard time keeping up.

He turns down one side street after another. Soon you are in a poorer and older part of the city. Some of the houses are little more than bamboo shacks. Despite the poverty, you notice that the streets are surprisingly clean.

The man increases his pace. You are almost chasing him now. He turns a corner. You race around the corner and run into a courtyard. But it's deserted—the man has disappeared!

Turn to page 52.

46

"EEEE YAA!" you yell, fists and feet flying into action.

The assassins are startled and hesitate. Your foot connects with the head of one at the same instant as your fist hits the dagger of another. The third drops his dagger and runs out of the room, only to be quickly captured by the guards.

The emperor wakes up screaming. Lin Fu calms him down. Dozens of warriors stream into the room. Lin Fu tells them all how you saved his father's life. They all bow respectfully.

The next day, the emperor holds a special session of the imperial court to honor you. He sits on a high jeweled throne in front of his glittering court.

"In gratitude and in recognition of your superior talents and courage," the emperor says, "I offer you the command of my armies."

Turn to page 33.

You go back to the freighter and reboard with Ling. It steams out of the harbor and down through a string of islands to the south, near the coastal island of Macao.

Just after noon, Ling points to an island nearby.

"Believe your friend held there," she says. "We there soon." She gives several orders in Chinese, and the kung fu fighters line up on the deck. They are wearing skin-diving equipment. Ling gives another order, and the fighters slip over the side of the ship and into the water.

One of the crew members leads you to a motorboat tied up alongside the ship. The two of you climb aboard and motor toward the island.

After you arrive, you find that the kung fu fighters have already captured a large group of Ninja and released a number of their prisoners.

You see Billy—dressed as a Ninja. Ling brings him over to you. He looks dazed.

"Your friend not real Ninja," she says. "Hypnotized and brainwashed. Couple of days everything okay. We fix."

Turn to page 107.

48

You decide to continue your search for Billy. It takes you over an hour to find the photo store.

"Hello. Anyone here!" you yell. No one answers. The store is deserted. You hear nothing except the rumble of traffic from the street outside.

A small movement toward the back of the store catches your eye. It's a beaded curtain rustling gently. It could be just the breeze, or *someone brushing against it!*

You walk to the curtain—and yank it open!

But there's no one there, either. It's only a storeroom. At the far end there's a door, slightly ajar.

As you walk toward it, a trapdoor opens under your feet, and you plunge downward!

Turn to page 55.

50

But you didn't come to the capital to sightsee. The Grand Master instructed you to find a boy named Lin Fu.

You ask the gate officer to take you to Lin Fu. He is startled by your request but does not object. He leads you to the palace. A small boy greets you.

"Are you Lin Fu?" you ask.

"*Prince* Lin Fu," the officer says, bowing very low. "This is the emperor's son."

You wait until the prince dismisses the guard before speaking. "I was afraid that I would arrive too late," you say, bowing. "The Grand Master sent me to warn you that the imperial court is filled with traitors. An attempt on the life of the emperor is near."

"We must go quickly, then," the prince says.

Turn to page 79.

"We have to get out of here!" you say, looking around the dungeon, "before whoever set this trap comes back to see who he's caught!"

You and Billy look around, trying to think of a way to escape.

"I have an idea," you say, snapping your fingers. "I can stand on your shoulders and try to reach the trapdoor. I can probably make it if we double up the mattress and you stand on that."

"Actually, I'd rather stay here and fight," Billy says, filling the air with kung fu kicks and hand chops. "I owe somebody for ruining our vacation."

If you try to climb out the trapdoor, turn to page 94.

If you decide to stay and fight, turn to page 76.

52

Bewildered and lost, you stand in the dim light of the courtyard. You see several wooden doors with dragons carved into them underneath a long curving balcony.

Suddenly several of the doors swing open at once. In a flash, you're surrounded by black-robed figures. One of them pulls a knife from beneath his robe and rushes at you, the knife pointing straight at your heart!

Turn to page 39.

54

You are angry and ready to fight when you reach the top. The guard roars with laughter. The "basket trick" is the biggest practical joke in the capital.

Relieved, you laugh with him. Better a practical joke than a gruesome death, you think.

You climb down a long ladder on the other side of the wall. The sight of the city on the way down takes your breath away. Wide boulevards and canals crisscross the city, which is illuminated by thousands of lanterns that look like fireflies in the dark, chilly night.

Horse-drawn carriages move up and down the streets—past small orchestras playing music, jugglers tossing flaming torches, and acrobats doing back flips and somersaults.

Turn to page 50.

You grab frantically at the edge of the floor near the opening, but you miss and land hard on a thick mattress.

Dazed by your fall, you sit and collect your senses and let your eyes adjust to the darkness. You rise shakily to your feet. The light is dim, but you can see that there's someone else standing in the shadows.

The figure emerges. You blink in disbelief . . . it's Billy!

"Billy!" you shout, embracing your friend. "What's going on here? Where have you been? What's happened?"

"Well," he says, "seems like we fell into some sort of trap. Yesterday I came into this shop chasing the guy who snatched my camera, and I ended up down here. But I don't know why we're here."

Turn to page 51.

One day, Han Shu is smiling broadly when you sit down in front of him for your lesson. "No more lessons. You now initiated in White Lotus Society. You must return to America at once and find this boy. He is a deadly and highly trained Ninja assassin of the Black Dragon Society."

You almost faint with shock when Han Shu shows you the photo. It's your friend Billy!

Turn to page 64.

58

The woman takes you to a small room on the second floor. You're a little disappointed that this room isn't nearly as nice as your room at the other hotel. An old mattress is pushed against one wall, with a mosquito net hanging over it. There's also a plain wooden table with two chairs in the other corner. Above you, an ancient ceiling fan slowly revolves.

"Toilet down hall," she says as she leaves.

You change your clothes and leave the hotel to go look for Billy. As you walk out the front door, a man walks briskly past you. You recognize him immediately—he's the man who stole Billy's camera!

If you follow the man, turn to page 45.

If you decide to return to the photo shop, turn to page 48.

You decide not to trust Fang. "I have a feeling if I stay with the tour, Billy will show up sooner or later."

"I think you make mistake," he says, "but be very careful—and good luck." He bows and leaves as suddenly as he appeared.

Your pulse quickens when you see Bob. He approaches you as if nothing has happened.

"Welcome to the tour," Bob says, enthusiastically shaking your hand. Then he leaves to re-join the rest of the group.

You don't know what to think of Bob's behavior. You doubt it was only a coincidence that at the same moment Bob disappeared, someone tried to kill you. Still, you have no proof and decide to give Bob the benefit of the doubt—for now.

Turn to page 102.

60

For the next month, you get up each day before dawn and join the society's kung fu masters and students in the temple hall for morning meditation. You have one simple meal of rice, vegetables, and some tea before noon.

After a week of this diet, you're dying for a slice of pizza and a soda.

When you're not meditating, your time is spent in martial arts training, as well as doing your share of chores: scrubbing the floor of the main hall, washing the walls, and picking beeswax out of Han Shu's honey jars.

You also have a philosophy lesson with Han Shu every day. "You must understand the Tao, the natural flow of energy in yourself, the universe— and in everything! Internal energy, very important, but most important of all," he says, concluding the lesson for the day, "make certain no beetles invade tomato patch."

Turn to page 57.

You watch as the man who rescued you pushes open a large door facing the courtyard. You follow him inside and down a long corridor. Before you reach the end of the corridor, he opens another door, revealing a stairway, leading down.

At the bottom of the stairway is a large, completely bare room with cement walls. There is a skylight overhead and a small door in one of the walls. Your friend talks to several men in white kung fu outfits. They step aside, and you go through the small door into the main hall of a large temple. It is lavishly decorated with gilded panels and carvings on the walls and ceiling. Kung fu fighters sit meditating on the highly polished wood floor in the center of the room.

Turn to page 90.

Bob takes the group on a tour of the temple's grounds. "The original temple was built on this site in the fifth century," Bob explains. "Here, a monk from India named Bodhidharma, or *Ta Mo* as the Chinese call him, taught his pupils how to meditate as well as perform the physical exercises that became the basis for the martial arts including kung fu, karate, and jujitsu."

You are fascinated by a beautiful garden you glimpse as you pass through a small arched gateway. A narrow gravel path winds its way down among a grove of old gnarled pines.

You leave the tour and walk into the garden. It's deserted. You walk down a winding path. Each bend brings another surprise: a small artificial lake, a shrine, a group of jagged rocks that resembles a miniature mountain range.

You see someone up ahead disappear around a bend in the path. You can't be sure, but it looked like Billy!

"Billy?" you shout, and run after the figure.

In your haste, you trip and hit your head on a stone. You feel the intense pain on your forehead before you black out.

Turn to page 67.

"But that's a picture of my best friend!" you shout in astonishment.

"I know," Han Shu says.

"But he's no assassin," you argue. "I mean, he cheats a little at checkers and throws an occasional spitball in our Little League games—but he's no killer!"

"Maybe friend change. After all, *you* change. Friend under evil influence of Black Dragon Society," Han Shu explains. "You find and bring back. Maybe we can help him. But must be very careful. Ninja master of brainwash and hypnotism. Maybe friend try to trick you."

"I'll do my best," is all you can think to say.

Turn to page 77.

You spring around. The man who pushed you is the same man who has been following you since Shanghai. He is looking around, trying to spot who threw the spear. Then you both see someone jump out from behind the figures of the spirit warriors. He moves so quickly you don't get a good look at him. In a second, he's out the door.

"Let's go after him!" you shout to the man who saved you.

"Hold on," he says, grabbing your arm. "You may get another spear for your trouble."

"Who are you?" you ask the stranger.

"My name is Fang Yeh," he says. "I am from the Central Security Office of the People's Republic—like your CIA. We think you might be able to help us."

"How?"

"We would like to use you as bait," Fang says.

"Bait!"

"As an American citizen in China, you can't be forced to help us. But you may prove to be most useful, and my country would be grateful."

"Yeah, but I might end up missing—like Billy," you say.

"But if you don't help us, we may *never* find your friend."

You don't know whether to trust this man, especially since his name is Fang.

If you decide to trust him, turn to page 74.

If you decide to stay with the tour and keep looking for Billy, turn to page 59.

You feel raindrops falling softly on your cheeks. Slowly you open your eyes. You see a group of orange-robed monks standing over you. They are splashing water on your face.

You try to shake the cobwebs out of your head as they pull you to your feet. You let your fingers slide up to the large bump where your head hit the rock. It stings painfully when you touch it. You start to run your fingers through your hair—but it's all gone. Your head's been shaved!

Astonished, you look down and see that you are wearing an orange robe, the same robe as the monks are wearing.

Turn to page 40.

68

"I'll join your society," you tell Han Shu.

"*Hun hao,* very good," Han Shu says, and bows to you. Awkwardly, you bow back.

Han Shu gestures for you to follow him. You walk down a long hall lined with doors. Han Shu stops and opens one of them. Inside is a tiny room with white walls and a window that looks like an upside-down, old-fashioned keyhole. The only pieces of furniture are a low cot and a small, square table with a lantern on it.

"This your room," Han Shu says, and closes the door, leaving you alone.

Even though the room is only a little bigger than your closet back home, it's comfortable. In fact, it's pretty cozy. You lie down on the cot. It's soft. For some reason you thought it would be like a bed of nails.

Han Shu comes back carrying a white kung fu outfit in one hand and a razor in the other.

"Must shave head. Then you put this on," he says, holding up the kung fu outfit. You figdet as he shaves off your hair. You hope you don't look *too* goofy and end up selling flowers at some airport. At least none of your friends are here to see you now.

Turn to page 60.

The heat hits you as you get off the plane. It feels like a hundred degrees even though it's night.

You walk through the terminal. In contrast to the bright lights and raucous noise in Shanghai, here in Sian everything is dimly lit and very quiet.

In the terminal, passengers from the plane are met by friends and relatives, all laughing and chattering happily. You go to the information booth—but it's deserted.

Feeling very lonely and out of place, you walk to the other side of the lobby and curl up on an empty bench. Using your bag as a pillow, you quickly doze off.

You open your eyes suddenly! That man who was in the tour office—he's staring down at you!

Turn to page 72.

You decide to go and protect the foreigners in the western provinces. You are put in command of a dozen Shao-lin fighters on horseback and ride west with them into the mountains. Your guide and right-hand man is a tough old Mongolian named Ochibal.

Several weeks later, you reach a small trading post by the edge of the desert near the Great Wall of China. You trade your horses for camels and pack them with supplies for a trip across the barren wasteland.

Suddenly Ochibal points toward a small cloud of dust on the desert horizon. His eyesight is as keen as an eagle's.

"Horsemen coming this way," he says. "Probably bandits."

If you prepare to defend the trading post, turn to page 97.

If you retreat back into the mountains, turn to page 88.

You jump up and look around, but the man has disappeared. You try to convince yourself that you were dreaming, but his image is crystal clear in your mind. It must have been him. But why is he following you?

It's getting light outside, and activity in the airport is picking up. Several planes take off at dawn. The lobby is filling up with people waiting for the next flight.

You go to the information desk and show the woman there the itinerary from the tour office. She smilies broadly and says, "Tour go to tombs, bus leaves in *two* minutes! You hurry!" she says, pointing to an exit at the far end of the lobby.

You reach the bus station just as the bus is pulling out. It's going down the street!

You run after it, waving your bag. The bus stops for you. You pay the fare and step inside. The bus is very crowded, so you have to stand.

The bus leaves the city of Sian and goes through the countryside. You see how people live here in homes cut into the sides of the rolling gray hills.

Finally the bus stops in front of a large, one-story building that covers the tombs.

Go on to the next page.

Your heart jumps as soon as you get inside and see your tour group. And there's no mistaking the sound of Bob's voice.

"Here in front of you are many of the six thousand life-size men and horses of terra-cotta that were made as a spirit army to guard the tombs," Bob explains.

As he lectures, you catch his eye. He stops talking in midsentence and stares at you as if he has seen a ghost.

Turn to page 82.

74

You decide to trust Fang. "I'll do anything I can to help," you say.

"Very good. Here's number one plan," Fang says. "When tour guide gets back, tell him that you feel sick and that you wait on bus. I'll explain why later."

Fang dashes off, leaving you alone. When Bob comes back, you tell him you feel sick and that you are going to lie down on the bus.

A few minutes later, Bob walks onto the bus, followed by the driver. There's no sign of the rest of the tour group, and Bob has an evil glint in his eyes. Then, as quickly as a panther, Bob springs forward, the edge of his hand slashing toward your throat.

Turn to page 81.

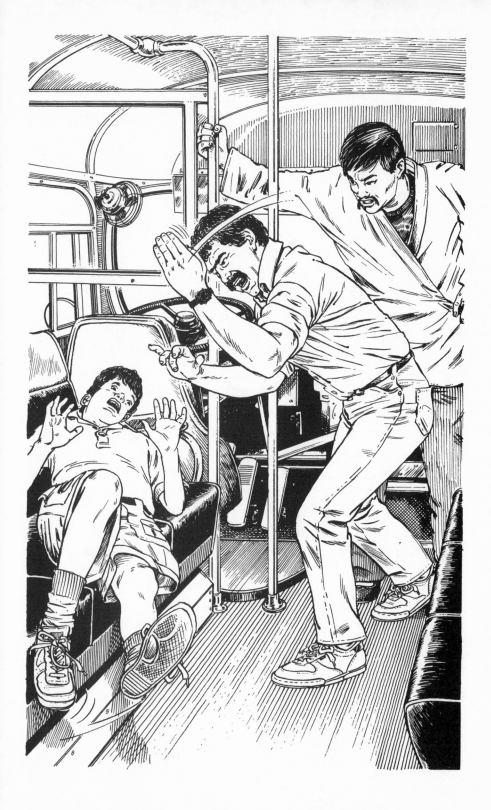

76

You and Billy are still arguing about how to fight your captors when you hear heavy footsteps on the floor above. You stand back in case someone falls through the trapdoor, but someone yanks up the door instead.

Then you hear hammering. Someone is nailing the trapdoor shut! Then the footsteps fade away.

A moment later, you hear pounding on the wooden door to your underground prison. "They're nailing the door shut, too!" Billy exclaims. He pounds on the door. "Let us out! We're American citizens!"

The hammering stops. You and Billy stand in the darkness. "What do we do now?" Billy asks desperately.

You look frantically about the room, seeking a means of escape. "Start digging," you say, kicking the dirt floor. "And let's hope we dig our way out of here fast—before we run out of air!"

You and Billy are galvanized into action. You dig to save your lives. You lose track of time, but eventually you dig your way into the other room.

You escape and take the next plane back home, wondering all the way who kidnapped you—and why?

The End

When you return to America a few days later, you find Billy. "The master of the White Lotus Society said that you'd become an assassin!" you shout, assuming a fighting stance. "You must return with me at once to China."

"White Lotus Society! Are you kidding?" he says. "They're the biggest bunch of murderers in the Far East. They're led by some nut named Han Shu. They kidnapped me our first day in China, but I escaped the next day and spent the rest of my vacation looking for you!

"I'm supposed to go back to China and be a witness against Han Shu, if they ever catch him," Billy continues. "That's probably why he wanted you to kidnap me and take me back." Billy shakes his head in dismay.

So it was all a plot by Han Shu to get you to kidnap Billy, you think, feeling embarrassed at having been tricked so easily.

Unless Billy's lying.

The End

You run after him down mazelike corridors in the palace. The prince summons the captain of the guard and as many warriors as he can muster along the way.

Lin Fu stops outside the bedchamber of the emperor. The door is slightly ajar.

"Where are the guards!"

You step inside. Several black-robed figures, daggers in hand, surround the bed. Their arms are raised to strike. Suddenly they notice you!

Turn to page 46.

80

"I'm waiting here for someone," you say, looking at the man suspiciously. You realize that this could be a trick to kidnap you just as Billy was kidnapped.

"There's no time for that!" the man says, impatiently tapping his walking stick on the shiny marble floor of the hotel lobby. "If you're coming, we must be off right now!"

You still don't move. The English man looks around nervously. Then you see one of the kung fu fighters from the ship heading your way. The English man sees him, too, and dashes for the exit. The kung fu fighter runs after him, and they both vanish into the night.

The figher doesn't return as you wait anxiously for Ling to arrive. Finally Ling enters through the front door and rushes over to you.

"We go!" she says. "Find friend. Make a big raid!"

Turn to page 47.

At that same moment, Fang and several kung fu fighters burst through the door of the bus and jump inside.

Bob stops his hand slash in midair. "Just teaching this new student a basic kung fu move," he lies, smiling sheepishly.

The bus driver bolts out the back emergency door. Kung fu fighters start to chase him, but Fang blocks them. "Let him go! We don't need him. We have 'Poison Claw' himself," Fang says, carefully approaching Bob, ready to strike a kung fu blow if necessary.

Bob pales at the mention of his code name.

One of the fighters escorts Bob off the bus and into a waiting police car.

Fang says, "We think Poison Claw responsible for disappearance of your friend—and many more like him. He leader of Ninja cult. Ninja kidnap, brainwash, and train young kung fu fighters to be assassins. He almost do same to you."

"But what about Billy?" you ask.

"Don't worry. I have men hidden outside. They follow bus driver back to hideout. Your friend will be rescued soon."

The End

"Keep looking at the exhibits," Bob instructs the tour group "I'll be back shortly."

You watch in amazement as Bob dashes through the exit. You chase him into another room. The room is full of tourists staring at figures of kung fu warriors holding spears.

Suddenly someone pushes you roughly as a spear whizzes by your head and embeds itself in the wall behind you.

If you hadn't been pushed out of the way, the spear would have hit you!

Turn to page 65.

84

You leave the hotel to go and find the police. You have a feeling that someone is watching and following you. You duck down a narrow alley. You take back streets until you get back to the main street.

Quickly you turn around! A man dressed in dark robes dives into a doorway.

You quicken your pace and walk down the main street. You find a traffic cop and ask directions to the nearest police station.

At the police station, you approach the front desk. "I'd like to talk to an investigator, please," you say to the officer at the front desk. "It's about a missing person."

"One moment please," the officer says. He has a short conversation on the phone. "Inspector Chan will see you. Second door down the hall on the left."

Turn to page 96.

You pack your suitcase, check out of the hotel, and go to the tour office. It's a long walk, and you get lost a couple of times. You think someone's following you, but you can't be sure.

Finally you reach the tour office and go inside. "Excuse me," you say to the secretary sitting at the front desk. "I missed the kung fu tour bus. Is there some way I could catch up?" you ask her, giving her your name.

"Oh yes . . ." she says, checking a list of names on a clipboard. "That's strange," she says. "You're not the only one who's missed the tour this time. And this has happened several times before on previous tours." The secretary seems lost in thought for a moment.

"Do you think I can still catch the bus?" you ask, trying to regain her attention.

"No problem," she says, ruffling through some papers. "It should be in . . . let's see . . . Sian tomorrow. We'll put you on the company plane flying there tonight."

While she makes out a boarding pass, someone enters the tour office. You turn around and— gulp—it's the man who has been following you!

Turn to page 100.

"I'll do it," you say. "I'll be your bait."

"Good!" Chan says. "Now, there no time to lose. Everything ready to go." Chan unrolls a large map of Shanghai onto his desk. He points to a spot near the center.

"This is Ruijin Street. My men already in position. All you do is walk down street." He reaches into his desk and pulls out a camera attached to a shoulder strap. "Wear this, look more like tourist."

You slip the strap over your shoulder. You leave police headquarters with Chan and take a police car to a corner near Ruijin Street.

"Just walk down street," Inspector Chan says, nudging you. "My best man only little ways behind you," he says, pointing to a man in a long dark robe.

"It's the same man who was following you before!

You walk down the crowded street. You stop to look in a few shops and to buy a slice of melon. You almost reach the end of the block when someone suddenly reaches out of a doorway and pulls you inside.

A smelly cloth is clamped over your nose.

You black out.

Turn to page 112.

88

You leave the camels, and remount your horses, and you and your band of fighters gallop back into the mountains near the village.

You make your way up the steep, treacherous mountain trail. Your horses keep slipping and sliding on the loose footing.

You order the fighters to dismount and lead their horses up the dangerous mountain path.

But when you finally reach the top, your horse is spooked by the scent of a mountain lion. It rears up and then kicks out! You grab the reins and try to calm the horse down, but the animal is too frightened. Its flank hits you and sends you flying over the side of the cliff.

As you are flying through space, you see a small pond among the rocks below. Your only hope is to land in the water.

You twist and turn as you fly through space. Just another foot . . . one more . . . and you can hit the water.

Turn to page 111.

"Something tells me not to," you say. "You can use someone else as bait."

"Then you must go home," Inspector Chan says. "Too dangerous to stay in China."

"But I haven't found Billy yet!" you protest.

"No can stay. Might get hurt," the inspector says, lifting the phone and making arrangements for your trip back home.

A month later you receive a phone call from Billy.

"Billy! Where are you? What happened?"

"I'm still in China. I got kidnapped by a Ninja cult. I escaped and went to the police, but I think they may have a spy on their police force. There's this one guy, Inspector Chan . . ." And the line goes dead.

The End

90

You stand there for a moment, openmouthed, staring at the scene. Your rescuer returns with an older man wearing a long, richly embroidered robe. He has a long straggly Fu Manchu mustache and wears a tall conical hat on his head.

"My name is Han Shu," he says. I am master of 'White Lotus Society.' We are a secret society that dates back hundreds of years. We welcome you into our ranks. You need only pass a certain period of training and initiation."

"If I join, will the society help to find my best friend Billy?—he's disappeared!"

"Yes," Han Shu says as if he already knows what you were going to ask him.

You'd like to believe him, but this could all be a trick.

If you decide to join the society,
turn to page 68.

If you decide not to join, turn to page 101.

You decide to take a chance that the food is not poisoned. Halfway through the meal you start to feel funny—as if all your energy is being drained from your body.

Then you hear an order from the Ninja leader. It's like an electric current running through your body. You jump to attention. You feel as if you're a puppet, controlled by invisible strings, without any willpower of your own.

Turn to page 23.

A month later, someone knocks on your door.

"Billy!" you shout. Your mouth hangs open in amazement as you stare at Billy standing on your front porch. His head is all bandaged up.

"You're not going to believe this," Billy says excitedly, "but after I chased the guy who stole my camera, I got hit by something—a bicycle or a trolley car. Ever since then, the inside of my head's been like a dark cloud. I have a hard time remembering things. And I have dreams that I'm being chased by Ninja."

You remember what you learned about Ninja—they use hypnotism, brainwashing, and even drugs on their victims.

And then you remember the bag of gold coins that Han Shu gave you.

The next day you and Billy are on a plane back to China. . . .

The End

94

"Let's try my plan to escape first," you say to Billy. "We have nothing to lose. If we get out, we can surprise whoever is responsible for setting this trap, and if we don't, we can stay here and fight."

"Makes sense," says Billy. The two of you double up the mattress. You take off your shoes and wobble onto Billy's shoulders.

You grope for the edge of the trapdoor, and push it up into the room. You manage to get a grip on it and pull up a little.

"Give me a shove!" you call down to Billy.

He grips your ankles and pushes you up just enough so you can pull yourself halfway up through the trapdoor opening into the room above.

The first thing you see is a figure standing in the dim light above you!

Turn to page 29.

96

You find the door and knock on it.

"Come in," a voice says.

Inspector Chan is a short man with a round bald head and a big smile that never seems to leave his face. "Glad you finally get here. Been expecting you for long time."

"You know who I am?"

"We know you come to China with friend and now friend missing. Many people missing who suppose to be part of tour. We try following you to see if someone grab you, too, but you keep giving us the slip."

"You mean you've known all along that Billy is missing!" you say, trying not to lose your temper.

"Know he is missing, but don't know where he is at. We hope you lead us to him. We use you as bait."

"Bait!" you yell in protest.

"Bait to set trap," Inspector Chan continues. "Somebody snatching kids off streets. Must find out why kids getting kidnapped. We need you to help us."

If you help them, you might end up missing like Billy.

On the other hand, you can't just leave Billy in China and go home.

If you agree to be bait, turn to page 87.

If you decide not to be bait, turn to page 89.

In preparation for defending the trading post, you hide your fighters in a few buildings. When the bandits arrive, intent on plundering the village, the element of surprise is on your side.

But there are too many of them. You are outnumbered five to one.

Suddenly Ochibal shouts something in Mongolian, and they all stop.

It turns out that the leader of the bandits is Ochibal's long lost brother. Ochibal points to you and speaks to his brother in Mongolian. "This is my friend, a skillful fighter and master of kung fu as well as a renowned teacher of the martial arts."

Teacher is the magic word. They take you and Ochibal back to the bandit stronghold. You live there the rest of your life, teaching the bandits the Shao-lin way of life.

The End

98

You lock yourself in your room and peek out through your window shade to see if anyone has been following you. The streets are dark and filled with shadows, but you don't see anyone watching the hotel.

After you make sure that the window is securely locked, you push your bed against the door. That way, if someone tries to get in your room while you're sleeping, you'll feel the bed move.

You take off your shoes and lie down on your bed with all your clothes on. You doze off.

You awake with a start! There's a Ninja in your room! You sit up in bed and feel the sweat trickling down your back. It was only a bad dream, you realize. You lie back down on the bed but don't sleep very well.

In the morning, you wash up and change your clothes. Sitting on the edge of your bed, you wonder what to do next.

If you decide to go to the police,
turn to page 84.

If you decide to try to catch up to the tour,
turn to page 85.

100

The middle-aged Chinese man who was following you says something to the secretary in Chinese. They argue loudly.

You quickly pick up your boarding pass and slip out the door. You hail a taxi right away, and this time no one seems to be following you.

The taxi takes you right to the airport. You show your boarding pass to a man at the desk, and he directs you to the far end of the terminal. You get in line with a group of Chinese businessmen waiting for the flight to Sian.

You board the ancient twin-propeller passenger plane, and the captain directs you to a seat next to a perfectly round, portholelike window. A fine mist of moisture fills the cabin as the plane's engines slowly sputter into action. Droplets of water fall from the roof of the plane.

You hope they can get this thing off the ground!

A few minutes later, the plane bounces down the runway and lifts into the air.

The humid atmosphere from the cabin and the steady vibration lull you to sleep. You wake up a few hours later as you land in the darkness of Sian.

Turn to page 69.

You decide not to join the society.

"I respect your decision," Han Shu says. "If you find friend, you may need this for trip back," he says, handing you a bag of gold coins.

"No offense, Mr. Shu," you say politely, "but if I get home in one piece, I'm going *camping* next summer!"

"Many lost sparrows return to nest," Han Shu says mysteriously. He bows and smiles benevolently at you.

Soon you are on your way back to America.

Turn to page 93.

The next stop on the tour is the interior of the house of a famous kung fu warrior who died in battle centuries ago.

You enter the house at the tail end of the tour group and keep an eye open for Billy—and any more of Bob's tricks.

You see a face at an open doorway. It looks like Billy!

You walk to the doorway and slowly push open the door. You see a long staircase leading down. You walk down the stairs and enter an underground tunnel lined with doors. One of the doors is open.

You walk through the door into a small room. Suddenly someone shoves you from behind, and you fall into a dirt pit! You lie at the bottom, dazed. The last thing you hear is Bob say to someone, "Wait till we leave, then fill it in."

The End

104

"I'd rather go back to the hotel and wait to see if my friend shows up," you say.

"As you wish," Chang Li says. "Ling will see that you get back safely to hotel," he says, bowing.

Turn to page 108.

You decide to wait till the morning to enter the capital. You walk away from the towering walls and down to the shore of a nearby lake. Its broad expanse gleams in the light of a half-moon just rising over the hills on the other side of the lake. Lights from fishing-boat lanterns dot the water's surface.

You lie down in a willow grove near the shore. You are dozing off when you feel a fishing net thrown on top of you. You open your eyes and see several soldiers pulling the net together—with you inside!

Turn to page 109.

106

You decide to wait an hour. Then, if Ling doesn't call, you'll go out to meet Billy.

As you wait by the phone, you wonder how Billy knew where to find you. You just arrived at the hotel minutes ago, and Ling and her grandfather were the only people who knew where you were going.

You doze off. The sun, streaming through the windows as it sets, wakes you up.

Soon it will be dark outside. You hope it isn't too late to meet Billy at Ocean Park. You just finish tying your shoelaces and are about to rush out the door when the phone rings. It's Ling.

"Meet me in the lobby of the hotel in an hour," she says, and hangs up.

You go down to the lobby and wait. You hope that since Billy knows where you are, he'll come here to find you when he doesn't see you at Ocean Park.

After a few minutes' wait in the lobby, you see an Englishman carrying a walking stick approaching you.

"Oh, there you are," he says. "Been looking all over for you. Your friend Billy sent me to fetch you. There's a car waiting outside for us and all that. Come along, now."

You should wait for Ling, but you don't want to miss what might be your only opportunity to finally find Billy.

If you go with the man, turn to page 17.

If you wait for Ling to show up, turn to page 80.

A few days later, Ling arranges for you and Billy to fly home from Hong Kong. You hug Ling good-bye and board the plane with Billy. The plane takes off, and soon you're thousands of feet above ground.

Billy sits quietly staring out the window.

You wonder what he's thinking about.

The End

"So sorry that you don't follow honorable grandfather's advice," Ling says, after you and she reach your hotel. "I would have liked to get to know American visitor better." She bows and leaves you wondering if you made a mistake in returning to the hotel.

Turn to page 98.

"This spy is disguised as a monk," one of the soldiers says.

"But I'm a humble monk—" you start to protest.

"Silence!" a soldier interrupts, poking you with his lance.

They toss you onto the back of a horse. You and the soldiers gallop into the hills. You come to a cliff. They pull you off the horse and drag you to the edge. You kick furiously, but you only tangle yourself in the net.

You scream as they throw you over the side of the cliff.

You feel yourself flying through the air. You try to look down, but there is only darkness.

Turn to page 111.

You wake up! Someone is splashing water on your face.

It's Billy!

"Billy!" You jump to your feet and stare at your friend in disbelief. Suddenly you feel dizzy from the crack on your head. Billy helps you to a bench in the garden.

"Billy!" you say again, overjoyed at finding your friend at last. "Where have you been?"

"I got lost chasing the guy who stole my camera. I couldn't find my way back to the hotel right away, and when I finally did, you were gone. I just caught up to the tour. Boy, am I glad to see you."

You must have had some kind of crazy dream, you realize. But the dream seemed so real, and it went on for so long. You've never had a dream like that before. It's almost as if you traveled back to a previous lifetime. But maybe all dreams are like that.

"Are you all right?" Billy asks, looking at you curiously. "By the way, what happened to your hair?"

"What's wrong with my hair?" you ask, carefully feeling the bump on your head.

Then you realize what Billy was talking about. Your head's been shaved!

The End

You wake up blurry eyed in a hospital bed. A nurse is standing over you.

As your eyes focus, you see Inspector Chan standing next to the nurse. The nurse says something to him in Chinese.

"She says you be okay," Inspector Chan says. "Thanks to you we catch whole bunch of kidnappers. Followed them when they take you to secret hideout."

"Who were they? Why did they take me and Billy?" you ask, sitting up in bed.

"Ninja!"

"Ninja?" you ask incredulously. "Why would Ninja want us?"

"Ninja kidnap young kung fu fighters and then hypnotize. They train you to be assassin!"

You breathe a sigh of relief at your close call and look forward to flying back home with Billy.

The End

You lead your armies north to attack the enemy. Equipped with the fire lances, they shoot their deadly metal pellets into the ranks of the enemy. The first enemy soldiers retreat in terror from the new weapons.

You are winning the battle when suddenly reinforcements attack you from the rear.

You gather the greatest kung fu fighters around you to counterattack, but it's too late. You're surrounded.

You turn around quickly and see an arrow hurtling through space toward you. *Thunk!* It embeds itself in your chest. . . .

"Oooohh . . ." you moan.

"You okay?" Billy asks, nudging you awake. "You were making some really weird noises."

"Must have fallen asleep," you mumble, rubbing your eyes and looking out the plane window.

"Well, you better fasten your seat belt," Billy says excitedly. "We're about to land in Shanghai!"

The End

ABOUT THE AUTHOR

RICHARD BRIGHTFIELD is a graduate of Johns Hopkins University, where he studied biology, psychology, and archaeology. For many years he worked as a graphic designer at Columbia University. He has written *The Deadly Shadow, The Phantom Submarine, The Secret Treasure of Tibet, Invaders of the Planet Earth, Planet of the Dragons,* and *Hurricane!* in the Choose Your Own Adventure series. In addition Mr. Brightfield has coauthored more than a dozen game books with his wife, Glory. The Brightfields and their daughter, Savitri, live in Gardiner, New York.

ABOUT THE ILLUSTRATOR

FRANK BOLLE studied at Pratt Institute. He has worked as an illustrator for many national magazines and now creates and draws cartoons for magazines as well. He has also worked in advertising and children's educational materials and has drawn and collaborated on several newspaper comic strips, including *Annie.* A native of Brooklyn Heights, New York, Mr. Bolle now works and lives in Westport, Connecticut.